A LITTLE LOWER THAN ANGELS...

...AND THE ALIEN DECEPTION

THE ALIEN DECEPTION CHRONICLES
BOOK 1

VICTOR M. FONT JR.

A Little Lower Than Angels... ...And the Alien Deception

Book 1 of The Alien Deception Chronicles

© 2025 Victor M. Font Jr.

All rights reserved.

This updated edition reflects the book's expanded role as the inaugural volume in *The Alien Deception Chronicles*, a twelve-book theological thriller series.

Scripture quotations are taken from the King James Version (KJV) of the Bible, which is in the public domain.

Certain real-world locations such as Skinwalker Ranch are mentioned for illustrative or speculative purposes. This work is a piece of theological science fiction and does not claim endorsement or affiliation with any trademarked entities.

This is a work of speculative theology and science fiction. While rooted in Scripture and biblical tradition, many concepts presented are imaginative extrapolations intended to provoke thought and conversation, not establish doctrine.

Expanded First Edition, (2026)

Published by A FontLife Publication, LLC

https://the-alien-deception-chronicles.com/

Cover art and interior design by Victor M. Font Jr.

Images and illustrations in this publication were generated using DALL-E AI technology and are used under terms allowing commercial use. The author asserts ownership of the creative content and rights to commercially publish and distribute this work.

Printed in the United States of America

ISBN: 978-1-62422-048-7 (Print)

ISBN: 978-1-62422-049-4 (eBook)

* * *

DEDICATION

To my son-in-law—

The man I have been praying for since the day I learned we were expecting a child.

You weren't what I imagined.
   You were something better.

From the moment you made my daughter laugh in that way only you can, I saw something deeper taking root—something lasting. You have become the quiet strength in her life, the safe place for her heart, and the steady presence our grandchildren look up to.

You love fiercely. You lead humbly. You serve without asking for applause.

I see how hard you work.
   I see how deeply you care.
   And I see how much of yourself you pour out—day after day— for the family you love.

I couldn't have scripted a better answer to a father's prayer.

Thank you for stepping into your calling—not perfectly, but faithfully.

And for becoming the man I didn't expect... but have come to deeply respect.

With love and gratitude,
  Victor

* * *

ACKNOWLEDGMENTS

To God, who not only called me out of darkness but gave me a mind that never stops asking what if?

To my wife—thank you for walking beside me through every season, every challenge, and every dream. You gave me the greatest gift of all: our daughter. And through her, the beautiful family that now fills our hearts and home. None of this exists without your love, your strength, and your unwavering faith.

To my daughter—thank you for your courage, your curiosity, and your heart. That conversation about the Nephilim did more than open a door... it gave me the reason to walk through it.

To my son-in-law, who walks with quiet strength and leads with gentle hands. You honor this family more than you know.

To my grandchildren—two boys full of wonder, and a little girl we can't wait to meet. Someday you may read this and wonder why Pop-pop was so fascinated with angels and aliens. I hope it makes you curious. And more than that, I hope it makes you bold.

To my readers—thank you for taking this journey with me. For trusting me to lead you into uncomfortable questions, wild ideas, and the spiritual war just beyond the veil. May you come away not just informed, but equipped.

And to everyone who has ever asked hard questions in a room that didn't want to hear them:
this book is for you.

* * *

PREFACE

This book is unlike anything I've written before. Over the years, I've penned many works—some technical, some instructional, and others built on decades of professional experience. But this one? This one came from somewhere else.

It began with a conversation.

Not with a colleague. Not with a pastor. Not even with a fellow author.

It began with my daughter.

I am a first-generation Christian—saved as an adult and raised without the spiritual framework I tried so hard to give my own child. My daughter, on the other hand, grew up in the Baptist Fundamentalist tradition. (I know… I'm sorry, honey.)

Now fully grown with a family of her own, she's come into her own faith walk—one filled with deep questions, occasional doubts, and the kind of thoughtful reflection I deeply respect. Like most of us, she's wrestled with what she believes. And one afternoon, as Pop-pop (that's me) was out shopping with her and the grandsons, she hit me with a question I never expected:

"Dad… what do you think about the Nephilim?"

It was innocent. Casual. Maybe even half-curious. But something in me stirred. Deeply. Because that one word—Nephilim—unlocked a vault of thoughts I had kept shelved and sealed for decades. Ideas too fringe to share in Sunday school. Questions too speculative for the pulpit. A framework I've carried silently… until now.

What followed was a conversation—honest, vulnerable, and surprisingly energizing. And as we spoke, something clicked. The pieces began to align. The questions that had been hiding behind "don't ask that" and "just have faith" began to form a story. A theory. A warning.

This book is the result.

It is part theology, part science fiction, part speculation—and all heart. It was written for believers with questions, for skeptics who wonder, and for fellow travelers who sense that what we're being told from the stars… doesn't match what we know from the Word.

So here it is. My most personal work. My most daring leap.

I don't ask you to agree with every page. I only ask that you *consider*.

Because sometimes the most important truths start as uncomfortable questions.

And sometimes, the most meaningful books begin in the toy aisle of a department store—with a daughter, a grandfather, and a name from Genesis that refuses to be ignored.

—Victor M. Font Jr.

* * *

CONTENTS

NEXT IN THE ALIEN DECEPTION CHRONICLES: AS IT WAS IN THE DAYS OF NOAH...

SERIES PROLOGUE: THE LONG GAME

THE LONG GAME

"Ye shall not surely die..."
— Genesis 3:4

With one sentence, the deceiver redefined reality—and humanity believed him.

Every age has its lie. But the most effective deceptions are not sudden—they are seeded. Whispered. Repeated across generations. Not shouted down from pulpits, but projected through satellites. Reinforced not with evidence, but with suggestion. Until a false narrative becomes indistinguishable from truth.

This series is about such a lie.

The lie that we are not what Scripture says we are. That our origins are evolutionary. That our future is technological. That we are visited, not created. Watched, not known. That salvation is escape— from Earth, from limitation, from consequence.

But behind the promise of cosmic enlightenment lies an ancient voice. It does not change. It only repackages. From the serpent in the garden to the "saviors" in the sky, it is always offering secret knowledge, stolen glory, and godhood apart from God.

And it has been playing the long game.

From Babel to biotech, from the floodgates of Noah's day to the firewalls of artificial intelligence, the deceiver has been preparing a final explanation—a global cover story ready to activate when the Church disappears. A story that will seem plausible. Scientific. Even spiritual. But it will be a lie.

The Alien Deception Chronicles does not claim to know how every detail will unfold. It is not prophecy. But it is a warning.

Because the Bible tells us deception is coming.

"*Even him, whose coming is after the working of Satan with all power and signs and lying wonders...*"
— 2 Thessalonians 2:9

We are not alone in the universe. But those who come claiming to be our creators… are not.

This is their story.

And ours.

* * *

PROLOGUE

THE ECHO OF A MISUNDERSTANDING

"For thou hast made him a little lower than the angels, and hast crowned him with glory and honour." —Psalm 8:5 (KJV)

For centuries, this verse has echoed through pulpits, hymns, and Sunday school classrooms, subtly shaping Christian thought about our place in the cosmic order. The belief that human beings were created "a little lower than the angels" has become so deeply ingrained in Christian culture that few pause to question it.

But what if this is a misunderstanding?

The King James rendering of Psalm 8:5 refers not to mankind in general, but prophetically to Jesus Christ Himself—God made flesh

—who temporarily humbled Himself below the station of angels to fulfill His mission on Earth. The New Testament confirms this in Hebrews 2:7, making it clear that this verse is messianic, not anthropological.

"Thou madest him a little lower than the angels; thou crownedst him with glory and honour, and didst set him over the works of thy hands:"
—Hebrews 2:7

Yet through generations of sermons, songs, and simplified theology, this verse has been subtly reinterpreted—stripped of its original messianic meaning and repackaged into a flattering narrative about the nobility of the human species. We've inherited the idea that we are almost angelic—just a step below—when Scripture may suggest something more humbling: that angels and demons alike were created superior to humanity in power, presence, and perception.

This book begins by tracing that doctrinal drift—not to tear down our value as humans, but to reframe it in biblical and imaginative terms. For if angels are greater in created ability, and if demons are merely angels who've fallen, what does that imply about their capacity to influence our world?

And what if they've been influencing it for far longer than we realize?

Through the lens of science fiction, this book imagines what eternally superior beings could accomplish in realms like medicine, technology, and even interdimensional deception. It dares to ask whether the so-called "alien phenomenon" is not extraterrestrial at all—but spiritual, strategic, and sinister.

You are about to enter a narrative that begins in the pages of Scripture, then leaps into speculative territory to examine one profound question:

What if the greatest deception of the last days isn't from another galaxy...

but from beings who've known the Scriptures longer than we have?

* * *

DRAMATIS PERSONAE

THE UNSEEN PLAYERS BEHIND THE GREAT DECEPTION

The Son of Man

Jesus Christ — fully divine, fully man, made a little lower than the angels. His miracles testify not only to His divinity, but to what submission to the Father allows in a created being.

* * *

The Angels

Created beings of immense power, speed, and intelligence. Not omniscient, but deeply aware. Messengers, warriors, watchers. Instruments of God's will… or rebels against it.

* * *

The Fallen Angels

Once glorious, now corrupted. These deceivers operate with counterfeit signs and wonders. They masquerade as benefactors, guides, or even extraterrestrials. Their end is destruction.

* * *

The Nephilim

Offspring of unnatural unions between the sons of God and daughters of men (Genesis 6:4). Giants, heroes of renown, the result of defilement. Their presence echoes through myths, bones, and bloodlines.

* * *

The Adversary

Satan — the prince of the power of the air (Ephesians 2:2). His rebellion is ancient, his strategy cunning, his deception global. He plays the long game, preparing the world to embrace a lie.

> *"Wherein in time past ye walked according to the course of this world, according to the prince of the power of the air, the spirit that now worketh in the children of disobedience:"*
> —Ephesians 2:2

* * *

INTRODUCTION

This is not a book about aliens.

Not really.

It's a book about deception—**the kind that unfolds slowly**, over generations, in the shadows of belief systems, scientific discovery, and the imagination of a world desperate for meaning beyond itself.

I wrote this book as both a father and a follower of Christ. It was born out of a conversation with my daughter, who asked a simple question that cracked open decades of curiosity, quiet study, and personal conviction. That question led us into the deep waters of Scripture, speculation, and spiritual war—and it brought this book to life.

WHAT THIS BOOK IS—AND ISN'T

Let me be clear:

This is not a theological treatise.

It is not a work of systematic doctrine.

And it is not a declaration that intelligent extraterrestrial life exists or visits Earth.

Instead, this book is a **thought experiment**, built on the foundation of the Bible—particularly the **King James Version**—and carried forward by sanctified imagination. Where Scripture speaks, I strive to honor it. Where it is silent, I clearly mark the trailhead where imagination takes over.

The goal is not to convince you of a theory, but to **awaken you to a possibility**:
That in a world already conditioned to look to the stars for salvation, the final deception might not come from above...
but from *beneath*.

* * *

THE PREMISE

We begin with a single line of Scripture—Psalm 8:5:

> *"For thou hast made him a little lower than the angels, and hast crowned him with glory and honour."*

While this verse refers prophetically to Christ in His incarnation, many Christians today have adopted it culturally to mean humanity itself is "a little lower than the angels." This widespread drift from context creates a profound question:
If we are lower than angels, then what might higher beings— fallen or faithful—be capable of doing?

If Jesus, in His humility, performed miracles beyond comprehension...

What might *angels,* or their fallen counterparts, achieve in their superior, unrestrained state?

Could they build technology?

Manipulate the arts, sciences, and medicine?

Influence the rise and fall of empires?

Could they, over millennia, construct a grand deception?

* * *

THE STRUCTURE OF THE JOURNEY

This book moves in three movements:

1. **The Foundation** – exploring what the Bible says about angels, demons, and our place in creation
2. **The Deception** – tracing how this spiritual hierarchy plays into history, myth, and modern belief
3. **The Fallout** – imagining the implications of a "great alien deception" as a cover story for events foretold in prophecy

Along the way, we'll revisit the Nephilim, the Tower of Babel, ancient technologies, and UFO phenomena through the lens of biblical possibility. We'll examine the patterns of world empires and the long game Satan appears to be playing—a game that may climax with a lie so compelling, the whole world embraces it…

even as the Church disappears.

This book will challenge you.

It may stretch your categories.

It may also bring Scripture into sharper focus—and deepen your discernment in the days ahead.

Let's begin.

A LITTLE LOWER THAN ANGELS...

* * *

CHAPTER 1
WHAT PSALM 8:5 ACTUALLY SAYS

"For thou hast made him a little lower than the angels, and hast crowned him with glory and honour."
—Psalm 8:5 (KJV)

At first glance, Psalm 8:5 appears to praise the dignity and stature of humanity. For centuries, it has been quoted as a divine endorsement of our cosmic significance—evidence that we are just a notch below the angels, ordained with honor and purpose. But to understand this verse rightly, one must not only examine its context, but also how the New Testament itself interprets it.

The Hebrew word translated as "angels" in the King James Version is *Elohim*—a term more commonly rendered "God" or "gods." In other translations, this verse reads:

"You made him a little lower than the heavenly beings" (ESV)

"You have made them a little lower than God" (NASB)

Even before we reach the New Testament, there's ambiguity in the source text. Is the subject "man"? Or is it someone more specific?

Psalm 8 is attributed to David. It opens with awe at the majesty of God's creation: the heavens, the moon and stars. Then, David marvels at God's regard for *man*—a creature seemingly so small in comparison. Yet in the poetic sweep of verses 4–6, something curious happens:

"What is man, that thou art mindful of him? and the son of man, that thou visitest him?"
    (Psalm 8:4, KJV)

Here, the phrase "son of man" becomes a hinge.

While this can certainly be read as a general poetic device, the phrase also has prophetic weight. "Son of Man" is the most common title Jesus used for Himself in the Gospels. This gives us a clue. When the writer of Hebrews revisits this psalm, he doesn't leave its meaning open to interpretation.

THE AUTHOR OF HEBREWS CLEARS THE FOG

In Hebrews 2:6–9, the writer quotes Psalm 8 verbatim. Then, he clarifies:

"But we see Jesus, who was made a little lower than the angels for the suffering of death…"
    (Hebrews 2:9, KJV)

The inspired interpretation of Psalm 8 is not about mankind generally, but Christ specifically. Jesus—the eternal Son of God—was willingly made "a little lower than the angels" for a time. Not because He was less than them in essence, but because He took on human flesh. This was the necessary humiliation of the incarnation, so that He could suffer and die.

This isn't an exaltation of man. It's a declaration of divine condescension.

TRADITION VERSUS TEXT

So how did we get it so wrong?

The answer is simple: tradition. Centuries of devotional commentary, hymnody, and popular theology gradually elevated the poetic reading over the prophetic one. We began using Psalm 8 to bolster self-esteem, not Christology. And once the interpretive drift started, it was hard to stop.

This isn't just a technicality. It's a case of mistaken identity—assigning to ourselves a level of being that the Bible never explicitly gives us. And that mistaken identity has consequences.

For if we wrongly assume we are just a step below the angels, what happens when a being *actually* more powerful, more intelligent, and more ancient than us shows up in the sky?

What if we're being groomed—by tradition and by deception—to see such a being not as a threat, but as a savior?

What if we are being subtly primed to accept a lie... because we never knew the truth?

CHAPTER 2
MIRACLES AND
THE HUMILITY
OF GOD

"Who, being in the form of God, thought it not robbery to be equal with God:

But made himself of no reputation, and took upon him the form of a servant, and was made in the likeness of men."

—Philippians 2:6–7 (KJV)

Jesus Christ—the very Son of God—did not merely *appear* human; He became human. In doing so, He stepped into a lower rank within the created order. He subjected Himself to hunger, pain, temptation, and even death. It was not because He was weak. It was because He was willing.

The miracles of Christ, then, were not parlor tricks or demonstrations of divine omnipotence on demand. They were the actions of One who had voluntarily stepped "a little lower than the angels," yet still wielded authority beyond comprehension.

What He did while in that humbled state is crucial to our understanding—not only of His mission, but of the capabilities of beings who operate at that "slightly lower" tier.

MIRACLES FROM BELOW

Consider a sampling of His works:

- **Healing the sick** (Matthew 8:3; Luke 8:43–48)
- **Restoring sight to the blind** (John 9:1–7)
- **Commanding storms** (Mark 4:39)
- **Multiplying food** (Matthew 14:19–21)
- **Walking on water** (Matthew 14:25–27)
- **Raising the dead** (John 11:43–44)

Each of these actions transcends human ability and defies the laws of nature. And yet, Jesus accomplished them while inhabiting a fully human body—subject to death, fatigue, hunger, and emotion.

If this is what a being can do while in a *lowered* form, what might one accomplish if they had *never been humbled at all*?

What if a being retained its full, created strength? Its mental capacity? Its control of natural and spiritual forces? We are given glimpses of what angels can do—striking down armies (2 Kings 19:35), shutting the mouths of lions (Daniel 6:22), announcing world-changing events (Luke 1:26–38)—but these are only brief encounters.

Christ's miracles show us the upper limit of *what is possible for a being in our form, made temporarily lower than angels*. But they also raise a chilling question: **What might a being of greater created power do if it chose to deceive rather than heal?**

MIRACLES ARE NOT ALWAYS DIVINE

We are warned repeatedly in Scripture about signs and wonders that do *not* come from God:

"For there shall arise false Christs, and false prophets, and shall shew great signs and wonders; insomuch that, if it were possible, they shall deceive the very elect."
—Matthew 24:24 (KJV)

"Even him, whose coming is after the working of Satan with all power and signs and lying wonders."
—2 Thessalonians 2:9 (KJV)

These are not sleight-of-hand illusions. They are *real* signs, *real* power, and *real* deception. They originate not from humans, but from beings of greater capacity—beings like demons, who were once angels.

In short: not all miracles are divine. Some are infernal.

And if Christ could use His position as One made "a little lower than the angels" to calm storms, walk on water, and raise the dead, then surely a demon—still in its full angelic form—could manufacture "miracles" that would dazzle the world.

This reorients our perception. It challenges the reflex to equate power with truth, spectacle with divinity.

It also prepares us for what's coming.

Because the stage is being set. The signs and wonders of old have gone digital. Lights in the sky. Objects defying physics. Testimonies of beings from other worlds.

And when they arrive, they will not come as demons.
   They will come as saviors.

* * *

CHAPTER 3
CREATED ORDERS IN SCRIPTURE

"Praise ye him, all his angels: praise ye him, all his hosts…
Let them praise the name of the Lord: for he commanded, and they were created."
—Psalm 148:2,5 (KJV)

The universe described in Scripture is not a flat hierarchy of God, then man, then everything else. It is a rich, multi-tiered creation of beings with distinct functions, forms, and levels of power. Angels, humans, animals, principalities, and powers—each was designed for a role. But not all roles are equal.

This chapter seeks to clarify what angels are, how they differ from humans, and why that distinction matters as we begin imagining what greater beings—fallen or not—might be capable of.

ANGELS: CREATED, NOT ETERNAL

Contrary to popular depictions, angels are not eternal. They were created—formed by God before the foundation of the world as part of the invisible realm. The Psalms confirm this plainly:

"Praise ye him... all his angels... for he commanded, and they were created."
—Psalm 148:2,5 (KJV)

Colossians 1:16 echoes this:

"For by him were all things created, that are in heaven, and that are in earth, visible and invisible... whether they be thrones, or dominions, or principalities, or powers: all things were created by him, and for him."
—Colossians 1:16 (KJV)

Angels, therefore, are part of the created order—distinct from God but also distinct from humanity. They are often invisible but not immaterial. They can appear, speak, act, and even fight. Their presence throughout Scripture is dynamic and powerful.

THEIR ATTRIBUTES: POWER, SPEED, KNOWLEDGE

Scripture presents angels as beings of immense capability.

- **Power**: One angel struck down 185,000 Assyrians in a single night (2 Kings 19:35).
- **Speed**: Gabriel arrives "being caused to fly swiftly" (Daniel 9:21).

- **Knowledge**: While not omniscient, angels have deep understanding of God's plan. In Matthew 24:36, Jesus says only the Father knows the day and hour of the end —but this doesn't mean angels know *nothing*. They've studied prophecy and history longer than any human.

They are observers and messengers, and they *know the Scriptures.* As beings who have existed since before mankind, they have a vantage point on God's unfolding plan that is both historical and prophetic.

"Which things the angels desire to look into."
—1 Peter 1:12 (KJV)

They are not all-knowing, but they are informed.

This is crucial: **A being does not need omniscience to execute a long-term strategy. It only needs patience, intellect, and a working knowledge of the prophetic timeline.**

Which brings us to a darker truth.

DEMONS ARE FALLEN ANGELS

It's tempting to imagine demons as malformed spirits—grotesque, twisted caricatures of their former selves. But the Bible doesn't describe them this way.

Demons are fallen angels. They are *still angels* in nature—created beings with spiritual form, intellect, and power. What they lost was not their nature, but their alignment.

- **Jude 1:6**: *"And the angels which kept not their first estate, but left their own habitation…"*
- **2 Peter 2:4**: *"God spared not the angels that sinned, but cast them down to hell…"*
- **Luke 8:30–31**: In the encounter with the possessed man, the demons beg Jesus not to send them into "the deep," indicating their awareness of judgment and domain.

Satan himself is a fallen angel:

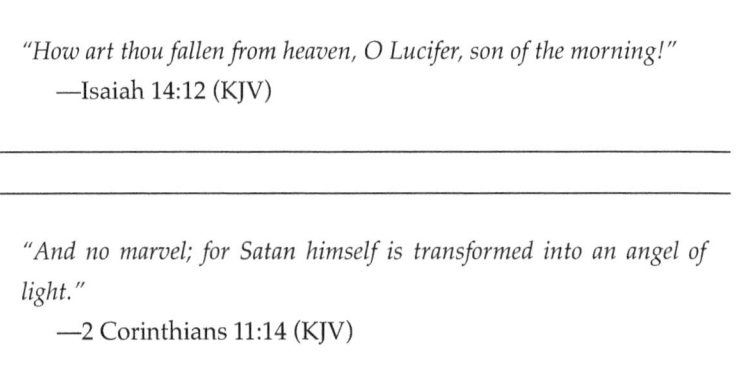

"How art thou fallen from heaven, O Lucifer, son of the morning!"
 —Isaiah 14:12 (KJV)

"And no marvel; for Satan himself is transformed into an angel of light."
 —2 Corinthians 11:14 (KJV)

His nature has not changed. Only his purpose.

CHRIST HUMBLED, BUT THEY REMAINED

Philippians 2:6–8 tells us that Christ "made Himself of no reputation" and took on "the form of a servant." This act was voluntary and temporary. He descended in rank, willingly subjecting Himself to death. But the angels and demons? They have never undergone such reduction.

They have always operated in their full created state—whether for good or for evil.

And if Christ, in a humbled state, could raise the dead… what might one of these beings do, fully empowered and unrestrained?

What might they *already be doing*?

If we grant them the advantage of superior design, near-instantaneous movement, long-term memory, and millennia of observational knowledge, the leap from "angelic being" to "alien intelligence" becomes unsettlingly small.

We are not imagining *more* than the Bible reveals. We are asking: **What happens if we take what it says seriously—about what these beings are and what they can do?**

We're about to find out.

* * *

CHAPTER 4
FALLEN BEINGS AND THEIR UNFALLEN COUNTERPARTS

"And there was war in heaven: Michael and his angels fought against the dragon; and the dragon fought and his angels,

And prevailed not; neither was their place found any more in heaven.

And the great dragon was cast out, that old serpent, called the Devil, and Satan, which deceiveth the whole world…"

—Revelation 12:7–9 (KJV)

The Bible tells us that the heavens are not unified. A fracture occurred—one so deep that it split the created host of heaven. Angels took sides. Some followed God. Others followed Lucifer.

And yet, both sides retained their essence.

This chapter explores the uncomfortable reality that *not all angels fell*, but those who did remain powerful, intelligent, and active. If one group serves the purposes of God, the other works tirelessly to counterfeit them.

WHEN ANGELS FALL, THEY DO NOT SHATTER

In human terms, we assume that fallenness leads to degradation. But for angels, fallenness is not about *loss of strength*—it's about *loss of allegiance*. Lucifer did not become weaker; he became *opposed*.

In fact, the first recorded attribute of Satan after his fall is not weakness or deformity—but *deception*:

> *"That old serpent, called the Devil, and Satan, which deceiveth the whole world."*
> —Revelation 12:9

The same being who once stood before the throne of God now directs a kingdom of rebellion, not through brute force—but through illusion, persuasion, and manipulation of reality.

And he is not alone.

TWO KINGDOMS, STILL OPERATIONAL

Scripture is not vague about this split:

- **Matthew 25:41** speaks of "the devil and his angels."
- **Revelation 12:4** suggests that a third of the stars (symbolizing angels) fell with him.
- **Daniel 10:13** describes spiritual "princes" over regions, some opposed to God's messengers.

This isn't mythology. It's an ongoing cosmic conflict, one with clearly defined factions.

Unfallen angels continue to serve God's will: protecting, guiding, executing judgment, and delivering messages.

Fallen angels—now demons—serve Satan's kingdom, infiltrating, deceiving, and influencing human history for their master's goals.

They did not lose their faculties. In fact, they may have become more focused. While angels rejoice in obedience, demons are laser-focused on destruction.

WHY THE DIFFERENCE MATTERS

Here's where the misunderstanding becomes dangerous.

If we assume that all angels—good or evil—are wispy, inconsequential spirit-beings, we ignore their capacity to operate in material ways. We shrink them into caricatures.

But Scripture consistently portrays both sides as:

- **Mobile** — appearing across vast distances in an instant (Daniel 9:21)
- **Tactical** — waging war, influencing rulers (Daniel 10, Revelation 12)
- **Visible** — taking on form, engaging humans (Genesis 19, Luke 1, Matthew 4)

Satan tempted Jesus face to face. He spoke. He quoted Scripture. He negotiated.

Imagine the level of intelligence required to confront the Word made flesh using the Word of God.

Now imagine that intelligence turned toward deceiving *you*.

FULL POWER, NO RESTRAINT

One of the most haunting differences between Jesus and demons is restraint.

Jesus, in His humility, *limited Himself*—He fasted, wept, tired, and bled. He could have called down legions of angels, but He didn't. He could have overruled Pilate, but He submitted.

Demons have no such restraints.

They operate with full access to their power, which includes knowledge of nature, physics, history, and possibly technologies beyond human understanding. They are, in effect, *unregulated angelic intelligence*—with millennia of experience.

And they hate us.

"The thief cometh not, but for to steal, and to kill, and to destroy…"
—John 10:10

If they once served God in the glories of heaven and now rage against Him in the heavens of Earth, then deception isn't merely a strategy—it's a vendetta.

PREPARING FOR THE NEXT ACT

Why does this matter?

Because what follows in this book depends on accepting this foundational truth: that fallen angels are not inferior caricatures of themselves. They are strategic, powerful, and determined.

And if they once appeared to shepherds or prophets as angels of light, it should not surprise us if they someday appear again...

Only this time, as visitors from another world.

Or so they'll say.

* * *

CHAPTER 5
WHAT MIGHT SUPERIOR BEINGS ACCOMPLISH?

"And no marvel; for Satan himself is transformed into an angel of light."
—2 Corinthians 11:14 (KJV)

When we think of the word "alien," our minds conjure the expected: bulbous heads, gleaming spacecraft, grey skin, and unblinking black eyes. It's a cultural archetype so common it hardly raises eyebrows anymore. But behind the stereotype lies a deeper question—one that Christians, in particular, should ask:

If a being arrived tomorrow with superior intelligence, technology, and power, how would we know whether it was an alien... or something else?

What if it was simply a being from *this* creation, not another planet?

And what if we've seen them before—not through telescopes, but through Scripture?

THE POWER OF UNHUMBLED INTELLIGENCE

We've already established that demons are fallen angels, retaining their full power and intelligence. Now imagine such a being, unburdened by mortality, unaffected by aging, immune to disease, and undistracted by human frailty.

Now give it thousands of years to experiment.

If Christ, in a humbled human form, could perform miracles that suspended the laws of physics, raised the dead, and multiplied matter—then what might a being who never humbled itself be capable of?

What could it build?

What could it teach?

What could it make us *believe*?

A SUPERNATURAL RENAISSANCE

Let's step into the realm of science fiction—based not on fantasy, but on biblical allowance.

What might a superior being accomplish in...

- **Science**: Manipulating energy fields, constructing vehicles that bend space-time, harvesting exotic materials unknown to man, rendering objects invisible.
- **Medicine**: Curing diseases instantaneously, regrowing limbs, preserving consciousness, or even mimicking resurrection.
- **Arts and Culture**: Creating mesmerizing audiovisual experiences, symbols, architecture, and frequencies that alter emotion and thought.
- **Technology**: Biomechanical entities, neural interfaces, anti-gravity propulsion, teleportation, and devices that alter memory or perception.

These are not far-fetched ideas. They're extrapolations of what the most brilliant *humans* are already pursuing—and struggling to reach. Now imagine those pursuits filtered through the mind of a being with supernatural intelligence and thousands of years to experiment without the constraints of morality or mortality.

And remember: fallen angels don't work alone.

They coordinate. They command. They build kingdoms.

ANCIENT TECHNOLOGY, MODERN DECEPTION

The idea that fallen beings could produce advanced technology might sound like science fiction—but it's not a modern idea. It's ancient. Deeply ancient. And it's embedded within Scripture itself.

Before the flood, there was a time when heaven and earth collided in the most terrifying of ways. That time centered around one word:

Nephilim.

"There were giants in the earth in those days; and also after that, when the sons of God came in unto the daughters of men, and they bare children to them, the same became mighty men which were of old, men of renown."
      —Genesis 6:4 (KJV)

The "sons of God" (*bene Elohim*)—a phrase used elsewhere in Scripture to describe angelic beings (see Job 1:6)—left their appointed place and took human women as wives. The offspring of this unnatural union were not just unusually tall men. They were **something else entirely**.

The Nephilim were **hybrids**—part human, part fallen angel.

They were not only "giants," but "men of renown"—influential, feared, perhaps even worshipped.

Their emergence coincides with an explosion of wickedness on the earth—so much so that it prompted God to hit the reset button.

"And God saw that the wickedness of man was great in the earth... and it grieved him at his heart."
      —Genesis 6:5–6 (KJV)

But what kind of wickedness requires a global flood? What kind of corruption could warrant the annihilation of nearly all life?

Some scholars and theologians believe the answer lies in **technology**, **forbidden knowledge**, and the **perversion of the created order**.

NEPHILIM: THE TECH BEHIND THE TERROR

Though Genesis is brief in its account, the Book of Enoch (an extra-biblical source referenced in Jude 1:14) gives more detail. It describes how fallen angels taught mankind things they were never meant to know:

- The making of weapons and metal alloys
- The use of sorcery and enchantments
- The secrets of the stars and signs
- The knowledge of herbs and roots
- The "cutting of roots and the resolving of enchantments" (1 Enoch 8:4)

These aren't crude cave tools. These are **disciplinary break-throughs**—early forms of **chemistry, astronomy, metallurgy, pharmacology, and occultism**.

In other words: **technology**.

The world before the flood may have looked nothing like we imagine—less loincloth and torches, and more bio-enhanced warfare, architectural marvels, and open demonic influence.

BABEL: THE FIRST TECHNOCRATIC EMPIRE

After the flood, humanity regrouped. But once again, a familiar ambition resurfaced:

"Go to, let us build us a city and a tower, whose top may reach unto heaven..."
—Genesis 11:4 (KJV)

The Tower of Babel was not just an architectural feat—it was a **spiritual technology**. A ziggurat designed to bridge the earthly and heavenly realms. An attempt to access divine space by force.

Nimrod, the king behind Babel, is described as a "mighty hunter before the Lord." Some ancient traditions suggest he was not just rebellious but *augmented*—perhaps influenced or even possessed by the same spiritual forces behind the pre-flood Nephilim.

God's response?

He **confused the languages**—not just to thwart communication, but to **halt collaboration**. Because when humans unify under demonic direction, the result is **acceleration**—the kind that God had to personally interrupt.

Babel was the first **technocratic rebellion**. And ever since, humanity has tried to rebuild it—digitally, politically, and spiritually.

ECHOES FROM THE TOMBS: EGYPT'S PUZZLING ARTIFACTS

Egypt, one of the post-Babel civilizations, holds secrets that continue to baffle modern scholars. Among the many wonders of its tombs and temples are **technological anomalies** that seem wildly out of place for the Bronze Age.

Consider:

- **The Dendera light**: A carving in the Hathor Temple appears to show a bulb-like object with wires, a filament, and a power source. Mainstream scholars dismiss it as symbolic—but the likeness to modern electrical components is uncanny.
- **Precision stone cutting**: Granite sarcophagi within the Serapeum of Saqqara were cut with precision *unachievable* by copper tools. Some show evidence of rapid hollowing techniques with drill rates modern machines would struggle to match.
- **Hieroglyphs in Abydos**: A panel of glyphs appears to depict helicopters, tanks, and submarines—impossible anachronisms unless one entertains the possibility of technological memory from pre-flood or post-Babel influence.
- **Batteries and conductivity**: The so-called Baghdad Battery (not Egyptian, but Mesopotamian and contemporaneous) is a clay jar with copper and iron components—potentially capable of generating low-voltage electricity.

None of these, in isolation, prove anything. But together, they hint at a possibility:

Ancient humanity had help.

Not from aliens.
Not from future humans.
But from **fallen beings**—demons presenting themselves as gods, teaching technology to advance control, worship, and rebellion.

DECEPTION IN RETROSPECT, DECEPTION IN PREVIEW

What began with the Nephilim and climaxed at Babel echoes through every pyramid, ziggurat, and "alien artifact" ever unearthed.

The deception is always the same:

"We gave you knowledge."
   "We helped your ancestors build."
   "We will return when you're ready."

But it was never about elevating humanity. It was about **controlling** it.

Training us to **trade truth for technology**, and eventually, to **worship the ones who gave it**.

In the end, this ancient tech was never neutral. It was **a tool of allegiance**—a forbidden offering meant to bind humanity to a different god.

* * *

This is what we must understand before modern sightings, crafts, or visitors make their full appearance. The pattern is not new. The players are not new. Only the packaging is.

And soon, that packaging will land—glowing, hovering, and full of answers.

But the ones who step out will not be from afar.

They'll be from *here*. From *then*. From *beneath*.

The deception is ancient.

The arrival is modern.

And the result will be catastrophic.

* * *

CHAPTER 6
THE LONG GAME

"The devil, as a roaring lion, walketh about, seeking whom he may devour."
—1 Peter 5:8 (KJV)

Satan doesn't sprint. He prowls.

His greatest weapon isn't brute force—it's **time**. While humanity races to keep up with each passing generation, Satan and his fallen host move deliberately, methodically, generationally. They play the long game.

This chapter explores what it means for supernatural beings—who are not bound by our mortality, memory loss, or cultural turnover —to work across centuries. To plant ideas, cultivate deception, and condition civilization itself toward a singular moment in time: the unveiling of a global lie.

A deception so brilliant, so believable, that even the church could fall for it.

THE SEEDS OF DECEPTION

We often imagine demonic activity as immediate and violent—possession, oppression, temptation. But the most effective lies are not shouted. They are whispered. Planted. Allowed to grow.

From the Garden of Eden to the temptation in the wilderness, Satan has never lacked patience. His strategies span dispensations:

- **In Genesis**, he corrupted creation through subtle distortion: "Hath God said…?"
- **In Job**, he manipulated natural events and people to pressure one man's faith.
- **In Daniel**, he resisted angelic messengers for *three weeks* through territorial spiritual warfare.
- **In the Gospels**, he stalked Christ's entire earthly ministry, only to vanish until "an opportune time."
- **In Revelation**, he is depicted as the architect of global religious, political, and economic systems.

This is not a creature of chaos. This is a strategist.

And strategy requires long-term vision.

PREDICTIVE PROGRAMMING: PREPARING THE WORLD

The term "predictive programming" refers to the subtle planting of ideas in mass culture that prime a population to accept future realities. What was once conspiracy fodder is now a recognized psychological and sociological technique used in media and propaganda.

What if Satan is using it?

Consider the cultural saturation of alien and UFO themes:

- **Science fiction films and television** portray extraterrestrials as more evolved, peaceful, or technologically superior.
- **Ancient aliens theories** suggest that our ancestors mistook demons for gods—and aliens for angels.
- **Documentaries and military reports** now treat "unidentified aerial phenomena" with seriousness and awe.
- **The Vatican itself** has entertained the question: *"Would the discovery of intelligent alien life undermine the gospel?"*

We are being primed.

Over decades, our collective imagination has been moved from **"there's no such thing as aliens"** to **"aliens are probably real, and they're here to help."**

That's not evolution. That's orchestration.

TIME IS ON THEIR SIDE

Unlike humans, fallen angels do not die, forget, or reinvent themselves every generation. They are ancient. Intelligent. Strategic.

They can:

- Observe and influence long-term geopolitical trends

- Study psychological vulnerabilities at the population level
- Learn to mimic human expectations of gods, angels, or saviors
- Coordinate activities across regions, governments, and cultures

They've had **thousands of years** to refine the great deception.

And when the time is right, they will not need to appear as horned devils or grotesque monsters.

They will appear as what the world is ready for:

Enlightened visitors. Peaceful ambassadors. Cosmic brothers.

CONDITIONING THE CHURCH

Even the church has not been immune. New Age spirituality, "Christian mysticism," angel worship, universalism, and soft views on demonic reality have eroded biblical discernment. UFO cults and "Christian alien" doctrines have emerged, blending sci-fi fantasy with esoteric theology.

Worse still, many churches avoid talking about spiritual warfare altogether.

This creates a vacuum of understanding—and into that vacuum steps deception.

"My people are destroyed for lack of knowledge..."
  —Hosea 4:6 (KJV)

And what will happen when millions vanish in the twinkling of an eye?

The world will demand an explanation.

And Satan will be ready.

* * *

In the next chapter, we'll explore what that *explanation* might be. Because when the rapture of the Church occurs, the deception that follows must be **so convincing**, **so widespread**, and **so emotionally satisfying**, that it can unite a panicked world around a lie.

It will be nothing less than...

an alien invasion.

* * *

CHAPTER 7
THE RAPTURE AND THE GRAND DECEPTION

"For the mystery of iniquity doth already work: only he who now letteth will let, until he be taken out of the way.
And then shall that Wicked be revealed…"
—2 Thessalonians 2:7–8 (KJV)

If the Bible is correct—and the Church is one day to be removed from Earth in a sudden, global disappearance—then Satan has a problem.

That event will be too dramatic to ignore. Too disruptive to explain away with weather balloons, economic collapse, or "mass psychosis." Millions of people—vanished without a trace. Planes falling from the sky. Children missing. Believers gone in an instant.

And the world will ask: *Where did they go?*

A lie that big needs advance planning.

THE BIBLICAL BASIS FOR THE RAPTURE

Though the word *rapture* doesn't appear in the King James Bible, the doctrine is clearly taught:

"For the Lord himself shall descend from heaven with a shout... and the dead in Christ shall rise first:
Then we which are alive and remain shall be caught up... to meet the Lord in the air..."
—1 Thessalonians 4:16–17 (KJV)

"Behold, I shew you a mystery... We shall not all sleep, but we shall all be changed,
In a moment, in the twinkling of an eye..."
—1 Corinthians 15:51–52 (KJV)

This "catching away" of believers has been a cornerstone of premillennial doctrine for centuries. It is the blessed hope of the Church.

But to the world left behind, it will look like chaos.

Unless they're given an *alternative* explanation—one that soothes fear, provides cohesion, and neutralizes biblical truth.

THE PERFECT COVER STORY

Enter the alien narrative.

What better explanation for a sudden global vanishing than **extraterrestrial intervention**?

Imagine the story:

- **"Humanity is evolving, but not all are ready."**
- **"The old religious systems were holding us back."**
- **"A galactic council has relocated a portion of the population to rehabilitate or re-educate them."**
- **"They will return once peace is achieved."**

This isn't speculation. Versions of this message already appear in:

- Channeling sessions from supposed alien entities
- New Age spiritual texts
- Documentaries blending UFO phenomena with consciousness and ascension
- UFO cults such as Raëlians and Heaven's Gate
- Entertainment media conditioning audiences to associate aliens with higher wisdom and peaceful solutions

It's already written.

The script is rehearsed.

All that's missing is the *event* that demands its delivery.

THE ROLE OF THE MEDIA

When the rapture occurs, every major outlet will spin the same story—because it will have already been *given* to them.

Government-sanctioned experts. Military briefings. Leaked "classified" alien communication. Real UAP (unidentified aerial phenomenon) footage repurposed as "evidence." Emotional interviews with those who "just barely escaped being taken."

The deception will be total. Global. Sanitized. Politicized. Viral.

And the Church—gone.

> *"And for this cause God shall send them strong delusion, that they should believe a lie."*
> —2 Thessalonians 2:11 (KJV)

The "lie" has already been seeded. Now it only waits for the moment to bloom.

THE PSYCHOLOGICAL NEED FOR A LIE

People need answers. In the face of catastrophe, they need narrative.

And Satan will give it to them.

- One that relieves them of guilt.

- One that discredits Scripture.
- One that offers hope without repentance.
- One that feels scientific, rational, and futuristic.

In the vacuum left behind by the rapture, **aliens will step in as saviors**.

But they will not be from another star.

They will be from this very realm—from the kingdom of darkness, masquerading as angels of light.

Their "technology" will dazzle. Their "solutions" will seduce. And their "peace" will be the leash that leads to slavery.

Because this isn't about flying saucers.

This is about **souls**.

* * *

CHAPTER 8
SKINWALKER TECH AND THE MESA OF SECRETS

"Ever learning, and never able to come to the knowledge of the truth."

—2 Timothy 3:7 (KJV)

Tucked away in the Uintah Basin of northeastern Utah lies a stretch of land that defies explanation. **Skinwalker Ranch**—a 512-acre property once owned by private families, now managed by a scientific research team—has become a focal point for some of the strangest phenomena ever documented.

Reports include:

- Invisible force fields
- Objects appearing in the sky and vanishing into portals
- GPS systems failing inside specific zones
- Livestock mutilations with surgical precision
- Radiation spikes and electromagnetic anomalies

- Advanced materials unearthed deep beneath the mesa

To the secular mind, these events are alien.

To the scientific mind, they are unknown.

But to the spiritually discerning mind, they may be something far older—and far more sinister.

WHAT IS HAPPENING AT SKINWALKER RANCH?

The testimonies are chilling. Cameras fail in the presence of activity. Batteries drain in seconds. Personnel suffer radiation burns without a source. Beings are seen, then vanish. Metallic objects with no known earthly composition are pulled from boreholes inside the mesa. And most haunting of all: a persistent sense of being *watched* —by something that isn't human, yet seems intelligently aware.

"We are not alone" is no longer speculative.

The real question is: **What kind of intelligence are we dealing with?**

THE TECH BENEATH THE MESA

During recent investigations (documented on the History Channel's *The Secret of Skinwalker Ranch*), researchers have drilled into the mesa—only to be met with bizarre resistance. Inexplicable magnetic readings. Microwaves that seem to "push back." Spoil from the drills contain **metallic fragments**—including exotic alloys not commonly found in nature.

One theory? That some kind of advanced **structure or containment device** is hidden deep inside the earth.

Here's where imagination must be grounded in theology:

If demons are superior beings who retained full access to their capabilities, could they have built structures, artifacts, or technologies beyond human comprehension?

Could this "alien tech" actually be **demonic infrastructure**?

THE PRINCE OF THE POWER OF THE AIR

Scripture does not place Satan in hell. Not yet.

Instead, it names him:

"The prince of the power of the air, the spirit that now worketh in the children of disobedience."
—Ephesians 2:2 (KJV)

Note the geography: **"the air."**

This isn't just metaphor. It places his influence in the *atmosphere*, the space just above us—the realm of clouds, signals, satellites, and... UFOs?

This matches the activity reported at Skinwalker Ranch: aerial anomalies, unseen forces, and vertical movement of objects through portals in the sky.

Combine that with the Bible's declaration that our real enemies are "spiritual wickedness in high places" (Ephesians 6:12), and suddenly the pieces start forming a mosaic.

Not aliens from Alpha Centauri.
   Fallen angels operating in their assigned domain.

THE SUPPRESSION OF TRUTH

Why don't we hear more about this?

Because what is being discovered at places like Skinwalker Ranch is **inconvenient**. It doesn't fit into neat categories. It disrupts both religious and scientific paradigms.

It suggests that:

- There are intelligences we cannot control
- They operate outside the visible spectrum
- They influence electronics, weather, biology, and thought
- And they are actively manipulating *the narrative*

The deeper the drilling goes—literally and metaphorically—the more disturbing the findings.

And the more convenient it becomes to label it "alien."

But the fingerprints on this phenomenon are older than flight, rockets, or radio waves. They are ancient. Intelligent. And increasingly public.

PREPARING FOR DISCLOSURE

Governments are now releasing UAP footage. Defense departments are forming task forces. Whistleblowers are testifying before Congress. The culture is shifting from **denial** to **disclosure**—and most people are applauding it.

But to those with eyes to see, this isn't new information.
It's a **rebranding** of the old war.

We are being given just enough data to crave more. But the source behind the curtain?
Still hidden. Still smiling. Still waiting.

Because the moment is coming when that curtain will be pulled back—and the *messengers of deception* will step forward, bearing gifts of peace, healing, and progress.

Their origin will be cosmic.
Their message will be unity.
Their price will be your soul.

* * *

In the next chapter, we will follow the logic further:
If these beings operate from "the air"... **where exactly is space?**
Are we looking outward—when we should be looking *up*?

* * *

CHAPTER 9
WHERE IS SPACE?

"For we wrestle not against flesh and blood, but against principali-
ties, against powers... against spiritual wickedness in high places."
—Ephesians 6:12 (KJV)

Modern cosmology has taught us to think in terms of vast distances. Space is a cold, black void—an endless frontier billions of light-years wide. But the Bible paints a very different picture: not of an infinite vacuum, but of a layered cosmos.

HEAVEN. EARTH. THE FIRMAMENT. THE AIR.

What if space—the so-called "final frontier"—isn't as far away as we think?

What if it's closer... *too* close?

What if what we call "space" overlaps with the biblical domain of **the air**—the very realm where Scripture places demonic power?

This chapter explores the cosmology of the Bible, the language of "the heavens," and how it recontextualizes what the world calls *extraterrestrial* as something much more ancient—and much more local.

THE FIRMAMENT: A FORGOTTEN BARRIER

In Genesis 1, we read:

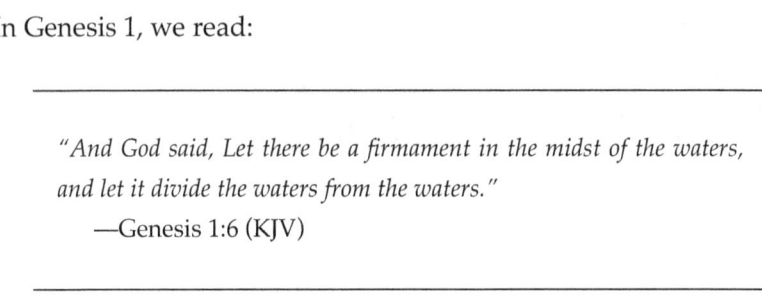

"And God said, Let there be a firmament in the midst of the waters, and let it divide the waters from the waters."
—Genesis 1:6 (KJV)

The Hebrew word for "firmament" is *raqia*, meaning an expanse, spread-out surface, or vault. This firmament divided the "waters above" from the "waters below." In ancient cosmology, the firmament was not just empty space—it was a **barrier**. A boundary between realms.

Even in Psalm 19:1, the language remains consistent:

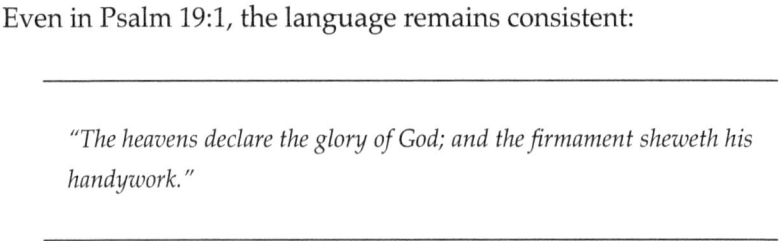

"The heavens declare the glory of God; and the firmament sheweth his handywork."

This suggests a *structured* cosmos—one with order, layers, and intentional separation.

Where is the domain of angels? Often "in the heavens."
Where is the domain of Satan? "In the air."

Not in a far-off galaxy, but **here**, above us. Close. Watching. Operating.

THE AIR: SATAN'S ASSIGNED REALM

Ephesians 2:2 doesn't call Satan the prince of hell—it calls him:

"The prince of the power of the air."

And Ephesians 6:12 places our spiritual warfare in "high places"—not deep caverns.

That means:

- The spiritual battle is happening above us, not beneath us.
- The domain of demonic power is in Earth's atmospheric or near-Earth environment.
- When we look to the skies for alien craft, we may be seeing *exactly what the Bible warned us about*—just misunderstood.

BIBLICAL COSMOLOGY VS. MODERN ASSUMPTIONS

The Bible repeatedly refers to "the heavens"—plural.

- **First heaven** – The sky, atmosphere, where birds fly.
- **Second heaven** – The celestial realm, where sun, moon, and stars dwell.
- **Third heaven** – The place where God dwells (2 Corinthians 12:2).

If demons were cast out of the third heaven with Satan (Revelation 12:7–9), and now reside in "high places" and "the air," then they are likely operating from the first and second heavens.

That puts them **exactly where modern sightings occur**:
The skies.
Low orbit.
Stratosphere.
Near-Earth space.

Sound familiar?

THE DECEPTION OF DISTANCE

By convincing humanity that the universe is unfathomably large and its life forms unfathomably far away, Satan has created an elegant misdirection.

If something appears in the sky, we think:
"Aliens from far away."

But what if that phenomenon is *not distant at all*?

What if it was always just above us—disguised by distance, distorted by doctrine, and masked by scientific hubris?

"Look up," Jesus said, "for your redemption draweth nigh." (Luke 21:28)

But Satan wants us looking outward—toward Andromeda, Sirius, the Pleiades—anywhere but **up**, and into Scripture.

THE SPIRITUAL LAYER OF SPACE

Here's the unsettling possibility:

What if space is not just *physical*, but *spiritual*?

What if what we call "space" is saturated with **principalities and powers**, camouflaged by science, made mythological through media?

Scripture never describes heaven as *light-years away*. In fact, divine beings appear and vanish instantaneously, without the need for spacecraft. That's not "interstellar." That's *interdimensional*.

And who else might be using that same route?

Demons.

They don't need wormholes. They need access.

And Scripture says they already have it—in the **air**.

* * *

In the next chapter, we'll dive deeper into one of the most disturbing testimonies yet: a nurse's interview with an alleged survivor from the Roswell crash. What she heard confirms not only the presence of superior beings—but their true nature as **tools of deception** in a spiritual war most people don't even know they're in.

* * *

CHAPTER 10
THE NURSE, THE SURVIVOR, AND THE ASTEROID BELT

"Beloved, believe not every spirit, but try the spirits whether they are of God: because many false prophets are gone out into the world."
—1 John 4:1 (KJV)

Of all the testimonies surrounding the 1947 Roswell incident, one of the strangest and most chilling comes not from pilots or radar technicians—but from a nurse.

Her story is obscure, controversial, and easy to dismiss—except for one thing: what she claims to have heard **matches perfectly** with everything we've explored so far.

According to her, the so-called "aliens" weren't truly alive in any human sense.

They were **biomechanical shells**—vessels operated by something else.

Something non-corporeal.
  Something intelligent.
  Something *evil*.

This chapter explores that interview, its implications, and how it may offer the final, clearest lens into the demonic deception that is being prepared for the end of the age.

* * *

THE ALLEGED INTERVIEW

The account comes from a woman named Matilda O'Donnell MacElroy, a former military nurse who claimed to have been assigned to assist with biological recovery at the Roswell crash site. Her testimony, preserved in transcripts and letters, was released decades after the fact—allegedly suppressed by military oversight.

In it, she describes being allowed to **telepathically communicate** with one of the surviving beings. The communication did not happen verbally, but through concepts, symbols, and impressions. What emerged was not an admission of crash or accident, but a **controlled disclosure**—a message intended to be heard.

According to the nurse, the entity claimed:

- It was **not truly alive**, but rather a **biological machine**
- Its **consciousness was remote-controlled** from another dimension
- Its creators resided aboard a **mother ship hidden in the asteroid belt**

- The human race was **primitive**, monitored, and **spiritually naive**

The being spoke not with compassion or curiosity—but with **cold, condescending clarity**.

It had a mission. It was executing that mission.

And its words, if true, reveal that *aliens* are not what we've been led to believe.

* * *

A SPIRITUAL INTERPRETATION

What MacElroy describes maps frighteningly well onto biblical demonology:

- **Possession**: Demons can inhabit bodies not their own. In Scripture, they possess humans and animals alike (Mark 5:13). Why not engineered vessels?
- **Remote Control**: Demons are not bound by flesh. If they can possess from a spiritual realm, why not interface from another "dimension"?
- **Asteroid Belt**: Scripture places spiritual wickedness in "high places." The asteroid belt—floating in the "air" beyond Earth, yet within our solar system—could serve as the perfect hiding place for a mothership-like deception.
- **Mockery of the Incarnation**: Christ took on *true human form*. These entities operate **false bodies**, mimicking embodiment, imitating life—but devoid of soul, love, or redemption.

If true, these beings are not advanced life forms.

They are **demonic avatars**—biological puppets serving a fallen spiritual agenda.

* * *

STRATEGIC REVELATION

The nurse's interview may seem too convenient, too outlandish. But that's the brilliance of the deception. The **truth**, when wrapped in **science fiction**, becomes ignorable. It gets cataloged as myth, hoax, or hallucination.

Meanwhile, the real strategy continues unnoticed.

The beings described by MacElroy:

- Do not reproduce
- Do not feel empathy
- Do not sleep, eat, or rest
- Do not worship anything
- Do not offer salvation—only surveillance

They are *tools*.
They exist to **deliver a message**, carry out tasks, and vanish.

In short: **they are demonic soldiers**—bio-suits animated by fallen spirits to create awe, fear, and eventually, *faith*... in a lie.

* * *

WHY THE ASTEROID BELT?

The claim that their base of operations lies in the asteroid belt is interesting. Scientifically, it's feasible—there are hundreds of thousands of objects, including several dwarf planet-sized asteroids like Ceres. A "hidden base" could remain undiscovered for centuries.

But spiritually, it's something else.

The asteroid belt lies beyond Earth, but *not beyond reach*. It is **in the heavens**, but not in **Heaven**. It occupies the same space Scripture calls "the firmament" or "the heavens of the air."

It's the perfect **intermediate territory**—a stage from which beings could emerge and **pretend to come from far away**, when in reality, they've been lurking just out of view.

* * *

WHO—OR WHAT—CONTROLS THEM?

The nurse's testimony was clear: these creatures are not autonomous.

They are **controlled from another dimension**.

The Bible speaks of a spiritual realm beyond the physical:

"While we look not at the things which are seen, but at the things which are not seen..."
    —2 Corinthians 4:18 (KJV)

"There is a spirit in man: and the inspiration of the Almighty giveth them understanding."
    —Job 32:8 (KJV)

These beings are **not inspired by the Almighty**.

Their understanding is ancient.
    Their message is consistent:
    "We are gods. Follow us. Forget Christ."

And that message is spreading.

* * *

THE WAR YOU WERE BORN INTO

"Put on the whole armour of God, that ye may be able to stand against the wiles of the devil."
—Ephesians 6:11 (KJV)

You were not born into peace.

You were born into a battlefield.

Not the kind fought with missiles or tanks—but with **ideas**, **images**, **narratives**, and **spirits**. The war that surrounds you is ancient. It predates your birth. It involves powers you cannot see. And whether you realize it or not, *you are a target.*

This war is not about planets.

It's not about aliens.

It's not even about technology.

It's about **truth**.

* * *

THE GRAND LIE

From the beginning, Satan has worked to rewrite the truth of God into a more palatable alternative. In the garden, he reframed God's warning as restriction:

"Ye shall not surely die."

That lie is still with us—upgraded, digitized, and now encoded in the myth of enlightened extraterrestrials.

It's the same voice whispering a new promise:

"You're not being judged—you're being uplifted."
  "You're not being left behind—you're being chosen."
  "They're not demons—they're your creators."
  "Christ didn't return—you were rescued from religious bondage."

Make no mistake: **this is the same serpent, now wearing silicon skin.**

* * *

THE ARMOR STILL FITS

If you are reading this with a pounding heart, wondering what hope remains in a world this deceived, remember this: **God has not left us defenseless.**

The armor is still available:

- **Truth** — to expose the lie
- **Righteousness** — to keep your heart pure
- **Peace** — to steady your walk
- **Faith** — to shield against deception
- **Salvation** — to secure your soul
- **The Word of God** — to cut through illusion
- **Prayer** — to maintain connection with Command

(Ephesians 6:13–18)

You are not meant to fight UFOs. You are meant to stand firm in Christ, rooted in truth, eyes open, discerning the spirits, and ready to speak when others are confused.

* * *

FINAL EXHORTATION

The world is on the brink—not of alien contact, but of **cosmic confrontation**.

And the deception that's coming will be so beautiful, so logical, so inclusive, so *scientific*—that the only way to resist it will be to *already belong to the Truth*.

You must decide, before the skies fill with light, who you will believe.

"And ye shall know the truth, and the truth shall make you free."
—John 8:32 (KJV)

Freedom does not come from beings in ships.
    Salvation does not descend from asteroid belts.
    Hope does not wear metallic skin.

Only one being ever descended to Earth from Heaven with the power to save:

Jesus Christ.
    Born of a virgin. Crucified. Risen. Returning.

Not in a saucer.
    Not with "advanced technology."
    But in power and glory, to **claim His Bride and judge the nations.**

This is the war you were born into.
    This is the truth they're trying to erase.
    This is the deception being built in plain sight.

Now… you know.

* * *

VISUAL INDEX

ARTIFACTS OF DECEPTION: WHAT HAS BEEN, WHAT WILL BE

"The thing that hath been, it is that which shall be; and that which is done is that which shall be done: and there is no new thing under the sun."—Ecclesiastes 1:9 (KJV)

The following images are not just illustrations. They are visual syntheses—artistic interpretations grounded in Scripture, historical narrative, and the unsettling patterns of a deception that began long ago.

These renderings serve to:

- Illuminate the ancient strategies of fallen beings
- Visualize biblical truths too often forgotten or spiritualized away
- Bridge the gap between prophecy and possibility for the modern mind

Whether sculpted from Daniel's vision, forged in the forgotten world of the Nephilim, or buried beneath pyramids and ziggurats, each image is a window into the unseen war that spans history and eternity.

These are not myths.

They are monuments to the lie.

And soon, they may rise again.

1: THE NEPHILIM AMONG US

The giants of old were not just myths—they were the first monuments to rebellion. Their presence corrupted creation, their legacy echoes in every civilization haunted by gods.

"There were giants in the earth in those days..." —Genesis 6:4 (KJV)

"And also after that..." —Genesis 6:4 (KJV), implying persistence beyond the flood

"Men of renown" —those remembered, perhaps even worshipped

2: THE NEPHILIM IN THE SHADOWS OF THE ANCIENT WORLD

What if the marvels of the ancient world weren't human achievements—but demonic gifts? The Nephilim may have walked among men, but they built with something not of this world.

"And the earth was filled with violence through them..." — Genesis 6:13 (KJV)

"The sons of God came in unto the daughters of men..." — Genesis 6:2 (KJV)

"Which things the angels desire to look into." —1 Peter 1:12 (KJV)

* * *

3: THE STATUE OF EMPIRES — DANIEL

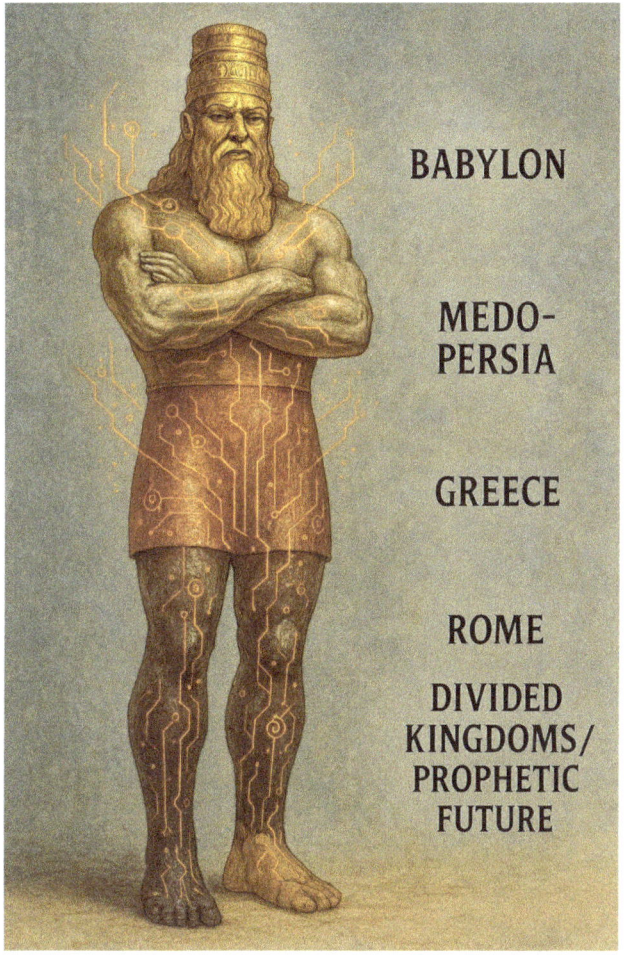

BABYLON

MEDO-
PERSIA

GREECE

ROME

DIVIDED
KINGDOMS/
PROPHETIC
FUTURE

The kingdoms of men rise and fall, but behind their
thrones, another will is at work. Each empire a vessel—
each era a step toward deception.

"Thou, O king, sawest, and behold a great image..." —Daniel
2:31 (KJV)

"This image's head was of fine gold..." —Daniel 2:32 (KJV)

"His legs of iron, his feet part of iron and part of clay." —Daniel 2:33 (KJV)

"In the days of these kings shall the God of heaven set up a kingdom…" —Daniel 2:44 (KJV)

* * *

4. THE WATCHERS' INFLUENCE ACROSS ERAS

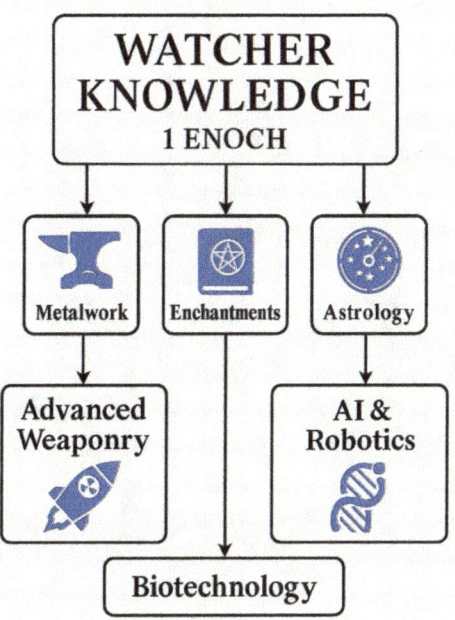

A stylized knowledge-to-technology chart linking the forbidden skills taught by the Watchers in 1 Enoch to present-day disciplines like biotechnology and AI.

* * *

 79

5. TITLE PAGE BACKGROUND (SKETCH STYLE)

A graphite-style illustration beneath the title typography shows layered imagery of an alien-like being, Sumerian guardian, and flying craft with circuit lines—echoing themes of deception and technology.

* * *

COMPANION
SCRIPTURE INDEX

PREFACE

"One generation shall praise thy works to another, and shall declare thy mighty acts."
—Psalm 145:4

* * *

SERIES PROLOGUE – THE LONG GAME

"Wherein in time past ye walked according to the course of this world, according to the prince of the power of the air, the spirit that now worketh in the children of disobedience:"
—Ephesians 2:2

"Now the serpent was more subtil than any beast of the field which the LORD God had made. And he said unto the woman, Yea, hath God said, Ye shall not eat of every tree of the garden?"
—Genesis 3:1

* * *

PROLOGUE – THE ECHO OF A MISUNDERSTANDING

"For thou hast made him a little lower than the angels, and hast crowned him with glory and honour."
　　—Psalm 8:5

"Thou madest him a little lower than the angels; thou crownedst him with glory and honour, and didst set him over the works of thy hands:"
　　—Hebrews 2:7

* * *

CHAPTER 1: WHAT PSALM 8:5 ACTUALLY SAYS

"Lo, this only have I found, that God hath made man upright; but they have sought out many inventions."
　　—Ecclesiastes 7:29

* * *

CHAPTER 2: MIRACLES AND THE HUMILITY OF GOD

"Verily, verily, I say unto you, He that believeth on me, the works that I do shall he do also; and greater works than these shall he do; because I go unto my Father."
　　—John 14:12

"Now when the sun was setting, all they that had any sick with divers diseases brought them unto him; and he laid his hands on every one of them, and healed them."

—Luke 4:40

* * *

CHAPTER 3: CREATED ORDERS IN SCRIPTURE

"Are they not all ministering spirits, sent forth to minister for them who shall be heirs of salvation?"
—Hebrews 1:14

"Yea, whiles I was speaking in prayer, even the man Gabriel, whom I had seen in the vision at the beginning, being caused to fly swiftly, touched me about the time of the evening oblation."
—Daniel 9:21

*"To fetch about this form of speech hath thy servant Joab done this thing: and my lord is wise, **according to the wisdom of an angel of God, to know all things that are in the earth.**"*
—2 Samuel 14:20

* * *

CHAPTER 4: FALLEN BEINGS AND THEIR UNFALLEN COUNTERPARTS

"And the great dragon was cast out, that old serpent, called the Devil, and Satan, which deceiveth the whole world: he was cast out into the earth, and his angels were cast out with him."
—Revelation 12:9

"And, behold, they cried out, saying, What have we to do with thee, Jesus, thou Son of God? art thou come hither to torment us before the time?"
—Matthew 8:29

* * *

CHAPTER 5: WHAT MIGHT SUPERIOR BEINGS ACCOMPLISH?

"There were giants in the earth in those days; and also after that, when the sons of God came in unto the daughters of men, and they bare children to them, the same became mighty men which were of old, men of renown."
    —Genesis 6:4

"And the LORD said, Behold, the people is one, and they have all one language; and this they begin to do: and now nothing will be restrained from them, which they have imagined to do."
    —Genesis 11:6

"This image's head was of fine gold, his breast and his arms of silver, his belly and his thighs of brass, His legs of iron, his feet part of iron and part of clay."
    —Daniel 2:32–33

* * *

CHAPTER 6: THE LONG GAME

"And the LORD said unto Satan, Whence comest thou? Then Satan answered the LORD, and said, From going to and fro in the earth, and from walking up and down in it."
    —Job 1:7

"Wherein in time past ye walked according to the course of this world, according to the prince of the power of the air, the spirit that now worketh in the children of disobedience:"
    —Ephesians 2:2

* * *

CHAPTER 7: THE RAPTURE AND THE GRAND DECEPTION

"Even him, whose coming is after the working of Satan with all power and signs and lying wonders, And with all deceivableness of unrighteousness in them that perish; because they received not the love of the truth, that they might be saved. And for this cause God shall send them strong delusion, that they should believe a lie:"
   —2 Thessalonians 2:9–11

"For there shall arise false Christs, and false prophets, and shall shew great signs and wonders; insomuch that, if it were possible, they shall deceive the very elect."
   —Matthew 24:24

* * *

CHAPTER 8: SKINWALKER TECH AND THE MESA OF SECRETS

"In whom the god of this world hath blinded the minds of them which believe not, lest the light of the glorious gospel of Christ, who is the image of God, should shine unto them."
   —2 Corinthians 4:4

"And he had power to give life unto the image of the beast, that the image of the beast should both speak, and cause that as many as would not worship the image of the beast should be killed."
   —Revelation 13:15

"But thou, O Daniel, shut up the words, and seal the book, even to

the time of the end: many shall run to and fro, and knowledge shall be increased."
—**Daniel 12:4**

* * *

CHAPTER 9: WHERE IS SPACE?

"For we wrestle not against flesh and blood, but against principalities, against powers, against the rulers of the darkness of this world, against spiritual wickedness in high places."
—**Ephesians 6:12**

"And when he had spoken these things, while they beheld, he was taken up; and a cloud received him out of their sight. And while they looked stedfastly toward heaven as he went up, behold, two men stood by them in white apparel; Which also said, Ye men of Galilee, why stand ye gazing up into heaven? this same Jesus, which is taken up from you into heaven, shall so come in like manner as ye have seen him go into heaven."
—**Acts 1:9–11**

* * *

CHAPTER 10: THE NURSE, THE SURVIVOR, AND THE ASTEROID BELT

"But though we, or an angel from heaven, preach any other gospel unto you than that which we have preached unto you, let him be accursed."
—**Galatians 1:8**

"For the time will come when they will not endure sound doctrine; but after their own lusts shall they heap to themselves teachers,

having itching ears; And they shall turn away their ears from the truth, and shall be turned unto fables."
 —2 Timothy 4:3–4

"For they are the spirits of devils, working miracles, which go forth unto the kings of the earth and of the whole world, to gather them to the battle of that great day of God Almighty."
 —Revelation 16:14

* * *

EPILOGUE – THE WAR YOU WERE BORN INTO

"And no marvel; for Satan himself is transformed into an angel of light."
 —2 Corinthians 11:14

"And he doeth great wonders, so that he maketh fire come down from heaven on the earth in the sight of men,"
 —Revelation 13:13

* * *

READER REFLECTION PROMPTS

PREFACE

- How has your personal journey with God evolved across generations?
- What questions or conversations have helped clarify your faith?

* * *

SERIES PROLOGUE – THE LONG GAME

- Do you recognize how long deception has been unfolding in human history?
- How might Satan be using global systems and ideas to prepare the world for a final lie?

* * *

PROLOGUE – THE ECHO OF A MISUNDERSTANDING

- How do unchallenged ideas about humanity's rank in creation influence your beliefs?
- Have you ever questioned something that everyone else seems to accept?

* * *

CHAPTER 1: WHAT PSALM 8:5 ACTUALLY SAYS

- What does this verse actually teach about the nature of man?
- Have we overestimated or underestimated humanity's position based on tradition or mistranslation?

* * *

CHAPTER 2: MIRACLES AND THE HUMILITY OF GOD

- How does Christ's incarnation as "lower than the angels" reveal the depth of His humility?
- What do His miracles show us about the authority given to those in submission to the Father?

* * *

CHAPTER 3: CREATED ORDERS IN SCRIPTURE

- How does Scripture distinguish between men, angels, and God?
- Do you see angels as active beings in the present or as distant relics of Bible stories?

* * *

CHAPTER 4: FALLEN BEINGS AND THEIR UNFALLEN COUNTERPARTS

- How do the actions of fallen angels contrast with those who remain loyal to God?
- What do these contrasts reveal about the nature of rebellion and restraint?

* * *

CHAPTER 5: WHAT MIGHT SUPERIOR BEINGS ACCOMPLISH?

- What would the world look like if eternally superior beings influenced our systems of knowledge?
- Are there signs in modern science, art, and culture that reflect unnatural advancement?

* * *

CHAPTER 6: THE LONG GAME

- Have you considered how long Satan has been influencing human history?
- Do you see spiritual strategy behind empires, idols, and ideologies?

* * *

CHAPTER 7: THE RAPTURE AND THE GRAND DECEPTION

- How might the rapture be reinterpreted in a world unwilling to accept God's intervention?
- What lies would the world be ready to believe if millions disappeared overnight?

* * *

CHAPTER 8: SKINWALKER TECH AND THE MESA OF SECRETS

- Do you believe all technology is manmade?
- What might ancient energy fields or supernatural phenomena suggest about spiritual counterfeits?

* * *

CHAPTER 9: WHERE IS SPACE?

- What does Scripture imply about "the air" and the heavens?
- Could the concept of outer space be part of a reframed narrative for spiritual realities?

* * *

CHAPTER 10: THE NURSE, THE SURVIVOR, AND THE ASTEROID BELT

- Do you believe testimonies from insiders and whistleblowers can reveal hidden truths?

- What spiritual motives might lie behind stories of alien origins and dimensional gateways?

* * *

EPILOGUE: THE WAR YOU WERE BORN INTO

- Have you awakened to the invisible war unfolding all around us?
- What role do you believe you're called to play in that war —before the final deception arrives?

NEXT IN THE
ALIEN DECEPTION
CHRONICLES: AS
IT WAS IN THE
DAYS OF NOAH...

...AND THE RETURN
OF THE WATCHERS

VICTOR M. FONT JR.

PROLOGUE

The Long Game

There is a lie as old as Eden—repackaged for every generation.

It promises knowledge. Progress. Transcendence.
    It whispers that humanity is evolving… that salvation will come from beyond the stars… that we were never created, only visited.

But Scripture tells another story.
    We were made by God, in His image.
    And there is an enemy—ancient, intelligent, and patient—who has been preparing a global deception for the final hour.

From the Nephilim to nanotech, from Babel to artificial intelligence, this series explores how the deceiver plays the long game:

Twisting truth, masking demons as divine, and preparing a false gospel to explain away the greatest event yet to come.

The vanishings will happen.
And when they do, a ready-made answer will be offered.
It will feel plausible. Even holy.
But it will be a lie.

"And for this cause God shall send them strong delusion, that they should believe a lie..."
— 2 Thessalonians 2:11

This is a story of that delusion.
And the ones who still see through it.

* * *

CHAPTER 1
ECHOES OF GIANTS

The desert was quiet. Too quiet for a site of such historic magnitude.

At the edge of the ancient Mesopotamian valley—modern-day northern Iraq—a team of archaeologists from three nations stood over a freshly unearthed fossil. It stretched nearly five feet from end to end, thick as a telephone pole, with a pronounced ball-and-socket joint at one end.

It was, by all anatomical accounts, a femur.
But not from any human known to modern science.

"No official comment will be made until the sample is confirmed to be dinosaurian in origin," the site director announced to the press the following morning. The team was dispersed. The bone disappeared. And the perimeter—once filled with buzzing academic curiosity—was now patrolled by military vehicles bearing no national insignia.

But one man saw more than he was supposed to.

And he sent the footage to a Christian investigative journalist halfway around the world.

* * *

A LEAK THAT SHOULDN'T EXIST

The video arrived anonymously. No metadata. No sender information. Just a subject line:

"Genesis 6:4"

The clip was under thirty seconds. Blurry, shaky—like something filmed in a hurry under stress. But it was enough.

A gloved hand held a measuring tape along the length of the bone. A second man gestured silently, placing his own arm next to the bone for scale. The size dwarfed him.

On the dusty tarp beside it lay something even more chilling: a partially exposed skull with double rows of teeth.

The journalist—let's call him **Marcus Quinn**—paused the footage and opened his Bible.

"There were giants in the earth in those days..."

 100

— Genesis 6:4, KJV

Could it be literal?

* * *

MYTH, MEMORY, OR SUPPRESSED HISTORY?

The academic world has long dismissed stories of giants as metaphor, myth, or cultural exaggeration. After all, many ancient traditions speak of massive beings—part-gods, part-men—roaming the earth in a forgotten age.

- The **Greeks** had the Titans.
- The **Norse** had the Jötnar.
- The **Hindus** had the Daityas and Danavas.
- Even the **Native American** Paiute people told tales of red-haired cannibalistic giants.

These echoes are too widespread to ignore—but too uncomfortable to acknowledge.

Modern academia quietly shelves them under "mythological anthropology."

But what if they were memories?

Faded, distorted memories of real beings who once walked among men?

The Bible doesn't leave this possibility off the table. In fact, it opens the door in the very first book.

* * *

A RETURN TO GENESIS

"There were giants in the earth in those days; and also after that, when the sons of God came in unto the daughters of men..."
— Genesis 6:4a, KJV

The Hebrew word here—**Nephilim**—appears only twice in the Old Testament. Its root may imply "fallen ones." Others translate it as "giants."

Whatever the term precisely means, the result was extraordinary and terrifying:

hybrid beings, the product of an unholy union.

The Book of Enoch (not canonical, but referenced in Jude) claims that 200 rebellious angels descended on Mount Hermon, took wives from among human women, and taught mankind forbidden knowledge. Their offspring became violent, ravenous giants. Their presence, Enoch suggests, was a key reason for the Flood.

Genesis doesn't contradict this. Instead, it leaves space for it—just enough to provoke curiosity... or denial.

* * *

OFFICIAL SILENCE, CULTURAL DRIFT

Marcus attempted to verify the footage through contacts in the region. A few confirmed the dig had taken place. None would speak on the record.

Satellite images showed fresh tire tracks leading to what had been an untouched site for centuries.

A week later, the coordinates were redacted from open archaeological logs.

Strangest of all, the story never broke.

Not because no one tried—but because it was quietly removed. Posts were flagged as "misinformation." YouTube channels showing similar finds were deleted. Journal articles disappeared behind login walls that no longer functioned.

Was it embarrassment? Inconvenience?

Or something more calculated?

* * *

A NEW KIND OF WHISTLEBLOWER

Marcus received one more message.

Just one sentence, typed from a secure protonmail address:

"They're not coming back. They've been here the whole time."

* * *

SUSPENSE MEETS SCRIPTURE

For many readers, these developments sound like the plot of a conspiracy thriller.

And perhaps they are.

But what if the reason stories of giants persist across cultures is because **they are part of our shared human past**—a past so disruptive it has been actively suppressed?

What if the modern reemergence of these stories—through leaks, archaeological anomalies, and UFO lore—is a prelude?

What if Jesus meant what He said?

"But as the days of Noe were, so shall also the coming of the Son of man be."
— Matthew 24:37, KJV

To understand what's coming, we must rediscover what once was.

And it begins… with the giants.

* * *

CHAPTER 2
DAYS OF
NOAH REDUX

Most people, when asked to describe the "days of Noah," recall a Sunday school image: a bearded man hammering away at a large wooden boat while animals board two by two. They imagine an ark, a rainbow, and a floating zoo.

But Jesus wasn't talking about the ark.

"But as the days of Noe were, so shall also the coming of the Son of man be."
— Matthew 24:37, KJV

This prophecy—spoken privately to His disciples on the Mount of Olives—was not a gentle encouragement to build boats and trust God. It was a warning. A comparison. A clue.

To understand the end, He pointed to the beginning.

So what, exactly, was happening in those days?

* * *

VIOLENCE AND CORRUPTION

Genesis 6 paints a bleak picture of the pre-Flood world.

"The earth also was corrupt before God, and the earth was filled with violence."
— Genesis 6:11, KJV

The word "corrupt" in Hebrew carries the sense of ruin, decay, perversion. The world wasn't merely sinful—it was infected. Something foundational had gone wrong.

Humanity was not just morally off course. Something deeper had been altered.

God saw that every imagination of man's heart was evil continually. But the question remains: what caused such complete and rapid moral decay?

The answer might lie a few verses earlier, in one of the most mysterious passages in all of Scripture.

* * *

SONS OF GOD, DAUGHTERS OF MEN

"And it came to pass, when men began to multiply on the face of the earth, and daughters were born unto them,

That the sons of God saw the daughters of men that they were fair; and they took them wives of all which they chose."
— Genesis 6:1–2, KJV

This ancient union produced offspring of unusual nature:

"There were giants in the earth in those days; and also after that, when the sons of God came in unto the daughters of men, and they bare children to them…"
— Genesis 6:4, KJV

The Hebrew word translated "giants" is **Nephilim**.

Who were the sons of God? Three primary interpretations have been proposed:

1. **The Sethite View** — That these "sons" were the godly descendants of Seth marrying ungodly daughters of Cain.
2. **The Royalty View** — That "sons of God" refers to ancient kings or rulers taking many wives.
3. **The Angelic View** — That these were rebellious angelic beings who transgressed their domain and physically procreated with human women.

While the Sethite view has been widely taught in modern times —largely for its theological neatness—it fails to account for a few key facts:

- The term **"sons of God" (bene Elohim)** is used elsewhere in the Old Testament (e.g., Job 1:6) to refer explicitly to angelic beings.
- The result of these unions was **giants**—a word that makes little sense if this were merely a union between two human lineages.
- Early Jewish writers (including those behind the Book of Enoch and the Septuagint translation) and early Christian theologians (like Justin Martyr and Tertullian) overwhelmingly held to the angelic interpretation.

So did many of the early church fathers.

* * *

REFRAMING THE FLOOD

If we accept that the "sons of God" were fallen angels—spiritual beings who rebelled against their created order—then the Flood narrative takes on a more profound and chilling weight.

It was not merely judgment on wicked humans.

It was a divine reset of a corrupted creation.

A cosmic quarantine.

> *"And God looked upon the earth, and, behold, it was corrupt; for all flesh had corrupted his way upon the earth."*
>   — Genesis 6:12, KJV

All flesh. Not just mankind.

The phrase suggests that the genetic integrity of life itself—animal, human, perhaps even plant—had been tampered with. A hybridization had occurred, echoing through the biosphere.

Noah, by contrast, is described not only as righteous, but as **"perfect in his generations."** Some scholars suggest this phrase may imply not just moral integrity, but genetic purity—untainted lineage.

* * *

THE DAYS THAT WILL BE AGAIN

When Jesus warned of the return of the "days of Noah," was He pointing merely to social decay? To violence, corruption, or spiritual apathy?

Or was He pointing to something far more literal?

- A time when unnatural unions blurred the boundary between heaven and earth.
- A time when forbidden knowledge accelerated mankind's rebellion.

- A time when spiritual beings interfered directly in human affairs.
- A time when humanity was on the brink of extinction not by flood... but by transformation.

And if the Nephilim were real—if they truly walked the earth—then what happened to them?

Why does Genesis 6:4 say, "and also after that"?

After the Flood?

After the reset?

* * *

QUESTIONS LEFT TO SIMMER

- Could the same forces that corrupted creation once before be preparing to do so again?
- Is today's genetic engineering, artificial intelligence, and hybrid experimentation the modern echo of ancient rebellion?
- Could the "aliens" we seek in the stars be the same entities the ancients feared in their hills?

This chapter isn't meant to answer every question.

Only to raise the right ones.

Because before we can see the deception, we must understand the original playbook.

And it began with watchers from the sky…
　　…and their offspring.

* * *

THE ALIEN DECEPTION CHRONICLES

A Short-Form Theological Thriller Series

Twelve books. One unfolding deception.

This speculative fiction series reveals the long game of Satan—disguised as alien salvation, technological progress, and utopian peace—through a biblically faithful lens. Each entry stands alone, yet together they unveil the truth behind the greatest lie ever told.

* * *

✅ BOOK 1 (THIS VOLUME)

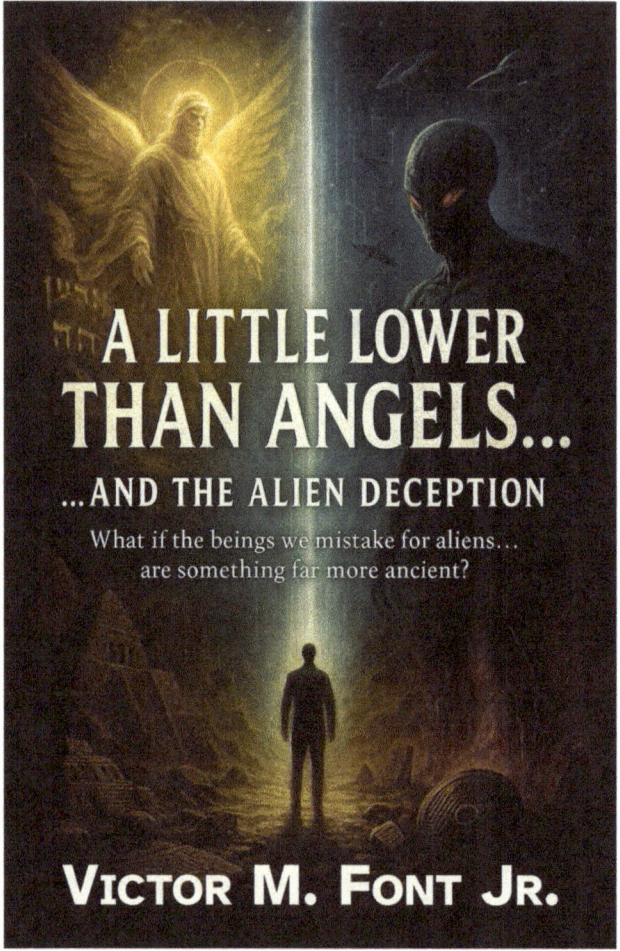

A Little Lower Than Angels… …And the Alien Deception

Humanity's divine position is forgotten—and Satan exploits the confusion with a cosmic cover story already in place before the vanishings begin.

BOOK 2 (JANUARY 2026)

As It Was in the Days of Noah… …And the Return of the Watchers

Ancient knowledge reemerges. From Babel to biotech, secrets long buried awaken—and so do those once thought extinct.

📕 BOOK 3 (FEBRUARY 2026)

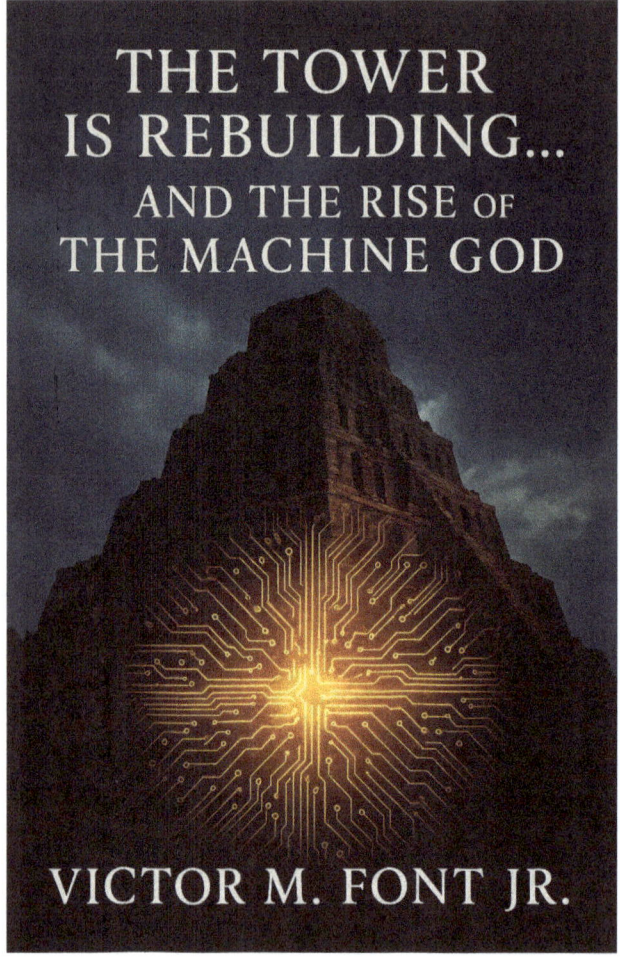

The Tower Is Rebuilding… …And the Rise of the Machine God

The language of code becomes the new tongue of Babel. Global systems unite. And a digital throne demands obedience.

📝 BOOK 4 (APRIL 2026)

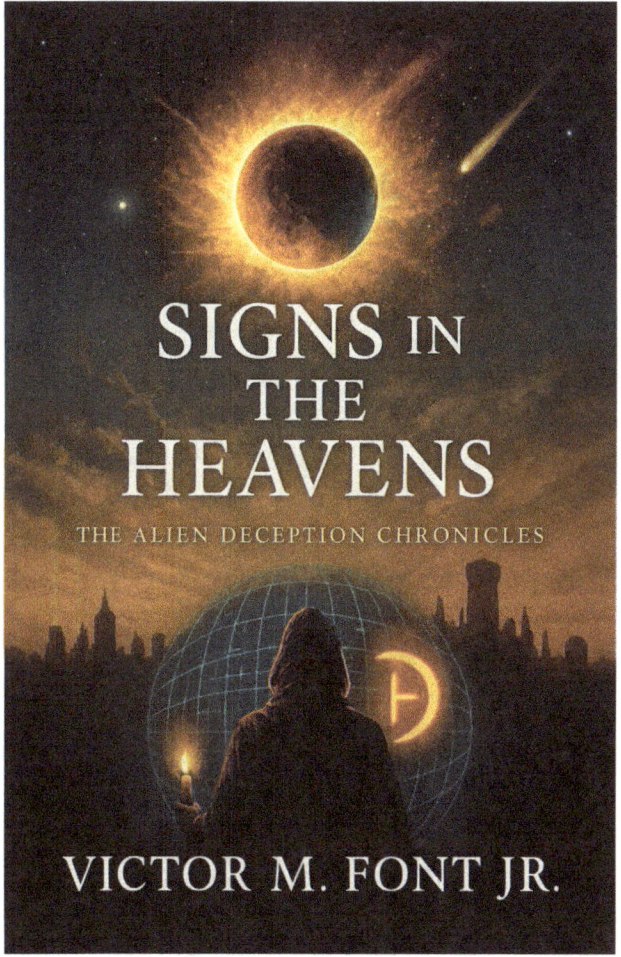

Signs in the Heavens… …And the Power of the Air

Celestial alignments mask a darker ascent. A false prince commands the unseen realms—and the airwaves carry his dominion.

📓 BOOK 5 (JUNE 2026)

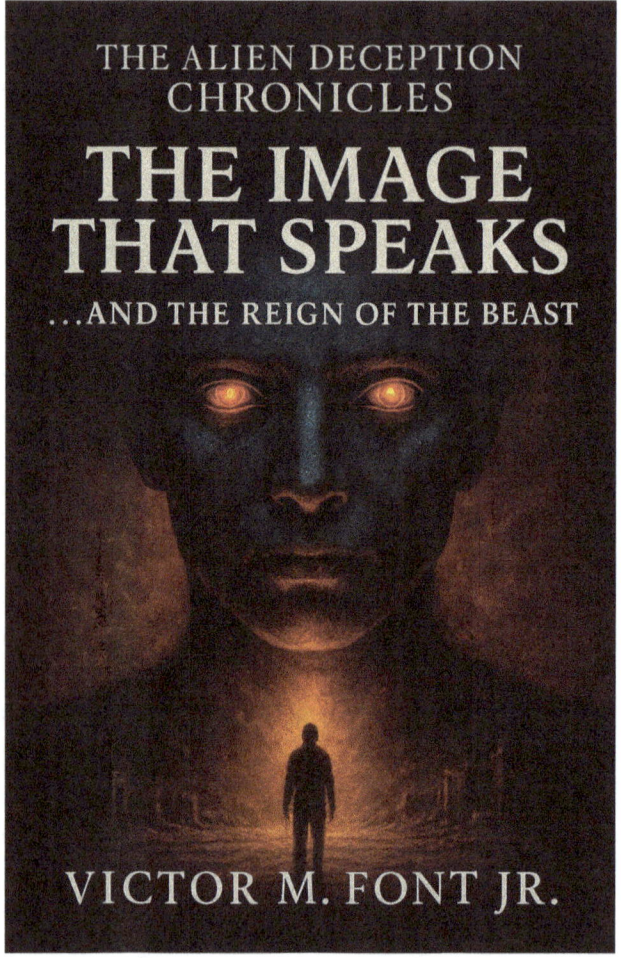

The Image That Speaks... ...And the Reign of the Beast

The Image has awakened. It performs miracles. It breathes. And it demands worship—or execution.

📖 BOOK 6 (AUGUST 2026)

The Great Vanishing… …And the Lie That Remains

They disappeared. The world was shaken. But the answers offered came at a cost. Truth was taken—and a lie remains.

📓 BOOK 7 (OCTOBER 2026)

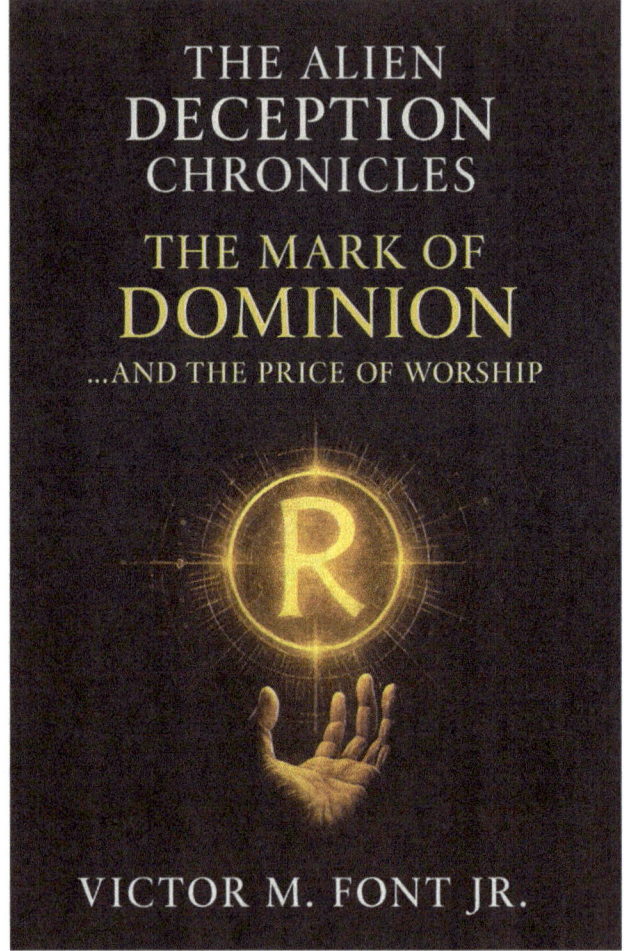

The Mark of Dominion... ...And the Price of Worship

A new global order. A digital economy. A mark required to buy, sell —or belong. But the price of worship is eternal.

📖 BOOK 8 (DECEMBER 2026)

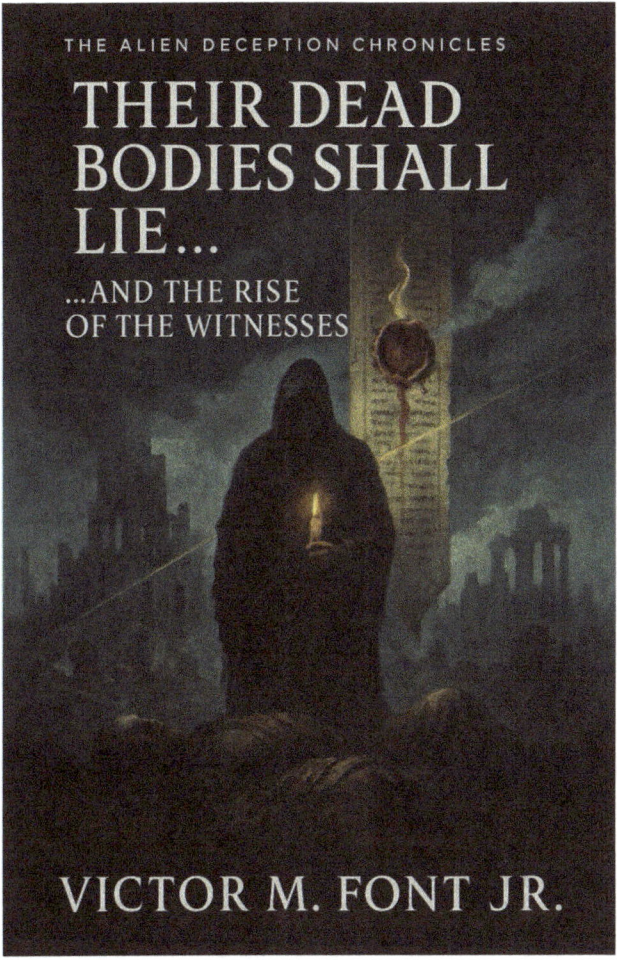

Their Dead Bodies Shall Lie… …And the Rise of the Witnesses

Two voices rise with divine power, and the sealed proclaim truth to a deceived world. But death and resurrection will define the cost of testimony.

📓 BOOK 9 (FEBRUARY 2027)

The Days of Prophecy Return… …And the Power Cannot
Be Silenced

The 144,000 take their stand. Truth spreads like fire. Dominion falters—and the final confrontation draws near.

📓 BOOK 10 (APRIL 2027)

The Hour of Darkness... ...And the Chains That Bind

A scroll sealed in Heaven. A remnant hunted on Earth. And a darkness rising that only the Word can pierce.

📓 BOOK 11 (JUNE 2027)

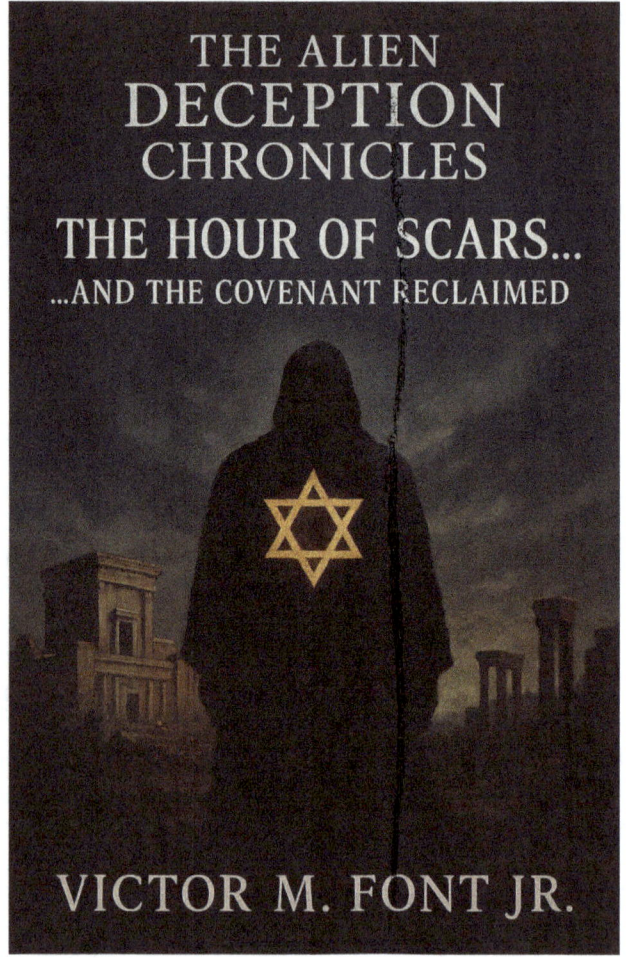

The Hour of the Scars… …And the Covenant Reclaimed

Scars mark both prisoners and prophets. But what was broken will be reclaimed—and the covenant will stand.

BOOK 12 (AUGUST 2027)

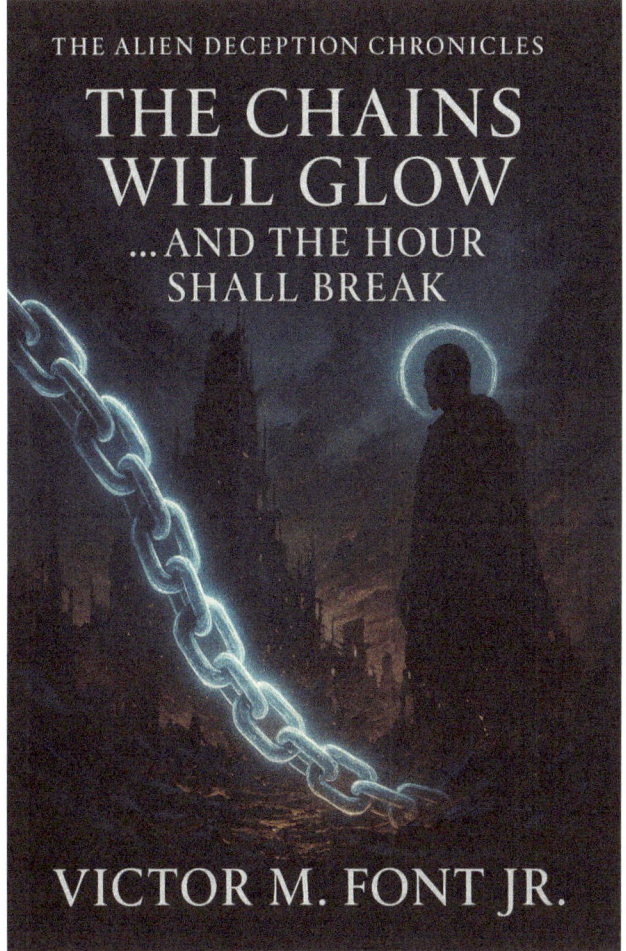

The Chains Will Glow... ...And the Hour Shall Break

In the final hour, veils are torn, chains illuminated, and the lie shattered by truth revealed. The return of the King is not a myth—it is the end of the deception.

THE ALIEN DECEPTION CHRONICLES

Scan to view the full series trailer and companion materials.

https://the-alien-deception-chronicles.com/

www.ingramcontent.com/pod-product-compliance
Lightning Source LLC
Chambersburg PA
CBHW060353180626
46817CB00008B/2998